For more information about the Ruby Who? short film and accompanying workbook,
please visit www.iliketobeme.com or email info@youcantbeserious.com.au

Illustrations by Alarna Zinn www.littlejanest.com

Special thanks to Patrick Dodson and Pause for E-fect Limited

ISBN 978-0-9876653-0-0

Published by Pause for Effect Limited
Printed by Lightning Source

National Library of New Zealand (Te Puna Matauanga o Aotearoa) data:
Title: Ruby Who?
Authors: Andrew & Hailey Bartholomew
Publisher: Pause for Effect
Address: 709 New North Road, Auckland
Format: Paperback
Publication date: March 2012
ISBN: 978-0-9876653-0-0

First Edition

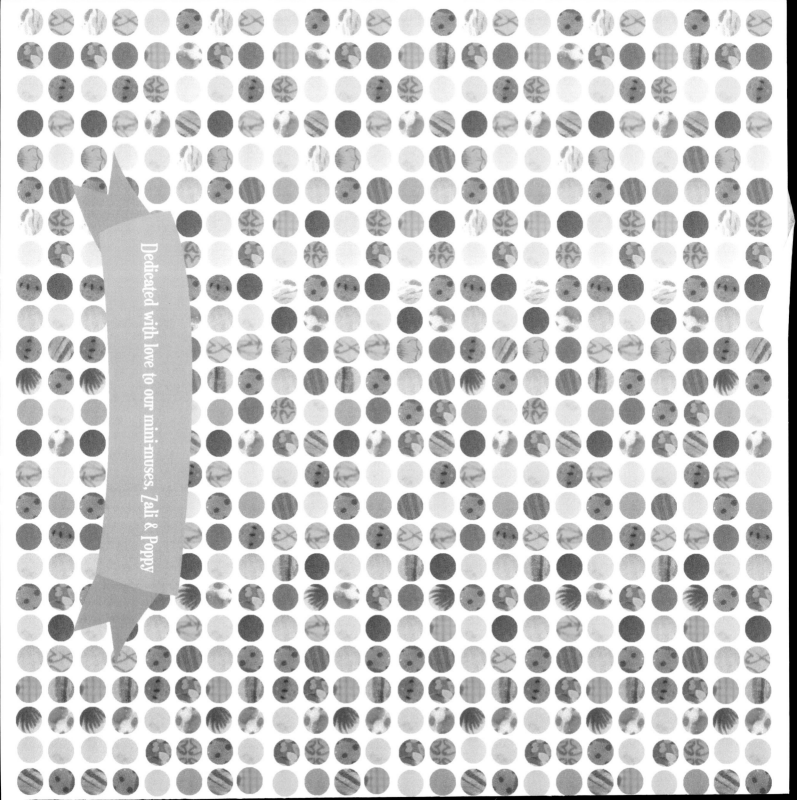

Dedicated with love to our mini-muses, Zali & Poppy

I am Ruby and this is Me.

I love twirly straws, buttons and beads.

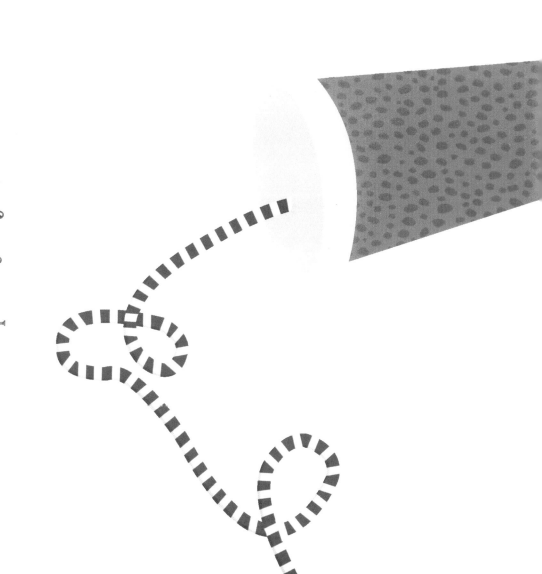

I like to dress up again and again...

'til Mum comes and says 'That's outfit number ten!'

But Mum, lots of outfits mean lots of fun!

Mum says I have a giant imagination.

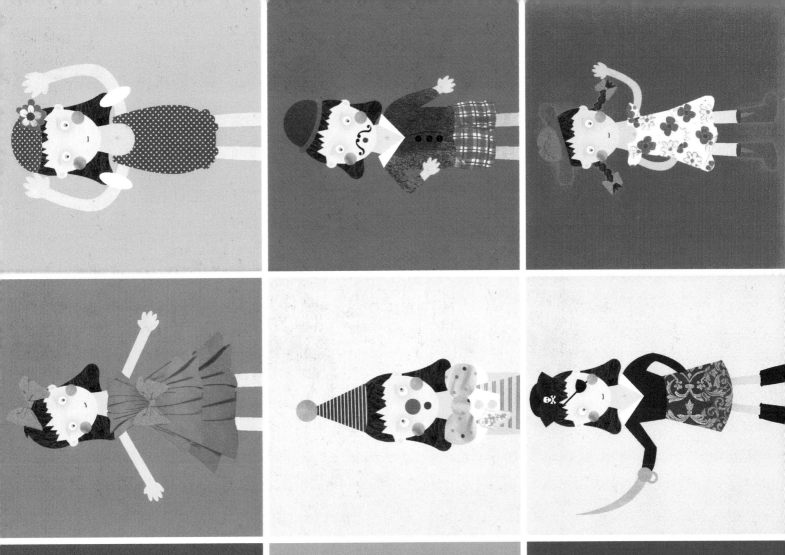
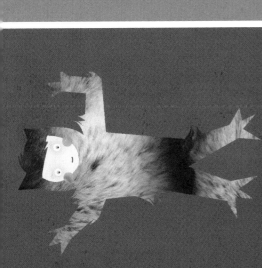
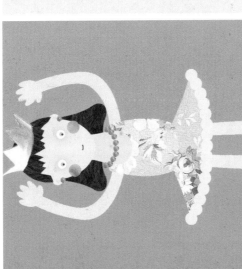

Mum and I walked to the park today.

Usually I hum and skip all the way…

But today something new caught my eye.

I couldn't look away – though I really did try!

A little girl with curls of gold.

Curls that were a wonder to behold.

Before I knew it I wished they were mine.

I blinked and suddenly it was my hair with a shine!

With a grin on my face I skipped beside mum...

When I spotted a girl with a smartie on her tongue.

It came from a cookie that was big and round,

I heard my tummy make a rumbling sound!

The little girl's coat was also appealing

It's huge red buttons gave me a funny feeling!

I wished that I too could look so fine

I blinked and cookie and coat were mine.

I was feeling very proud
of my cool new things,

When I noticed a blue tutu
and some sparkly wings.

Though happy with all
I'd been given before,

I just couldn't stop
myself wishing
for more!

I blinked and to my delighted amazement

The tutu and wings arrived in an instant!

The magic had worked once again it was clear

I had no need for anything else to appear!

But maybe there still was a gap in my life

I thought as I watched a young boy zoom by...

His roller skates carried him at high speed

I blinked - these were something I need!

The trick seemed again to work out a treat

As my eyes darted down to my freshly clad feet

For there in a blur of leather and steel

Gleamed the world's fastest shoes on wheels!

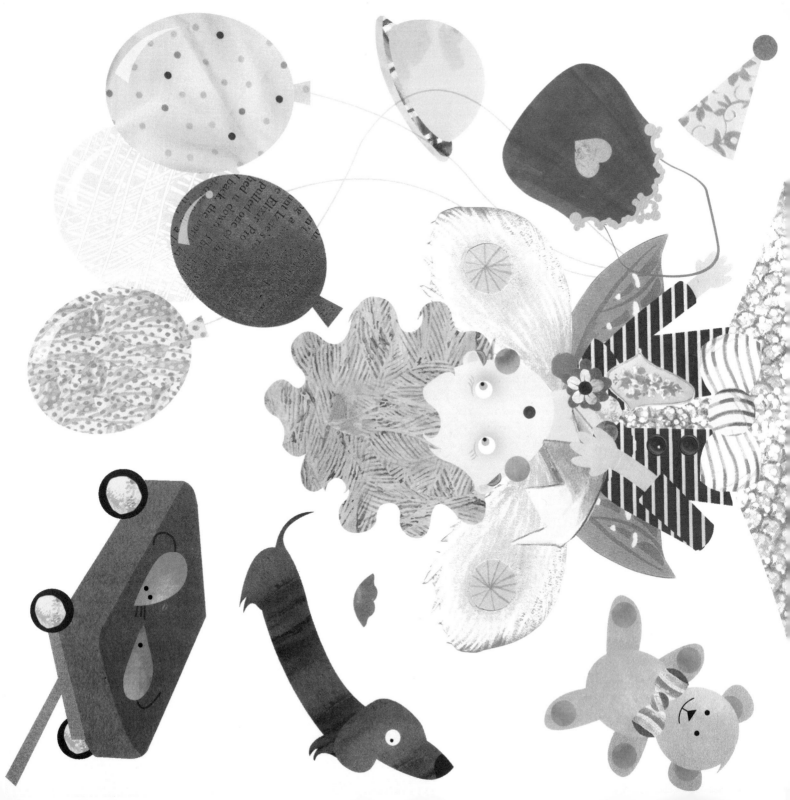

I started to feel a little despondent –
Wherever I looked I saw things that I wanted!

Rosy red lips and pretty handbags.

Giant balloons and stuffed toys and hats.

A little red wagon would be quite nice...

An umbrella, some freckles, a puppy, two mice!

I could no longer skip - even skating was slow,

When I got to the park I knew something must go!

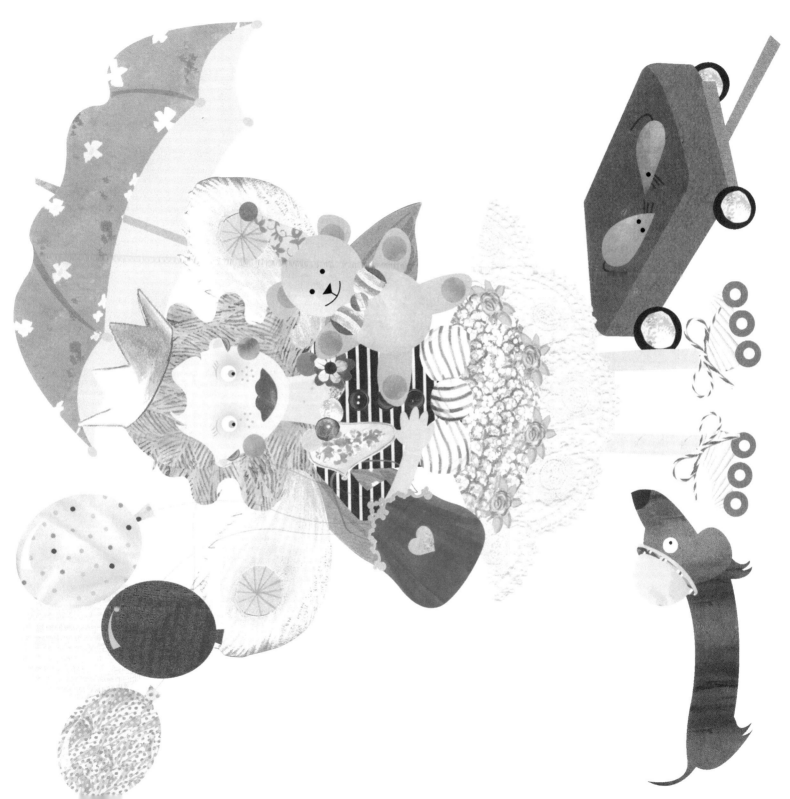

I sat on the grass
and I looked at the swing.

Maybe I don't need these
roller skate things!

They're clumsy and clunky
and hard to skip on

I looked at my feet.

and the skates were all gone.

Come to think of it these wings, this tutu and coat

Are becoming less fun than I firstly had hoped.

As this thought crossed my mind I stood up and cheered

What I once thought I needed had now disappeared!

I was feeling much lighter and freer, but wait -

There were still so many things in my way.

I had to let go and I didn't shed a tear.

Just let me keep my shiny blonde hair!

I ran to the swing – nothing slowing me down.

My feet touched the sky as I soared from the ground.

Never felt so alive – so glad to be me.

Surely there was no better way to be.

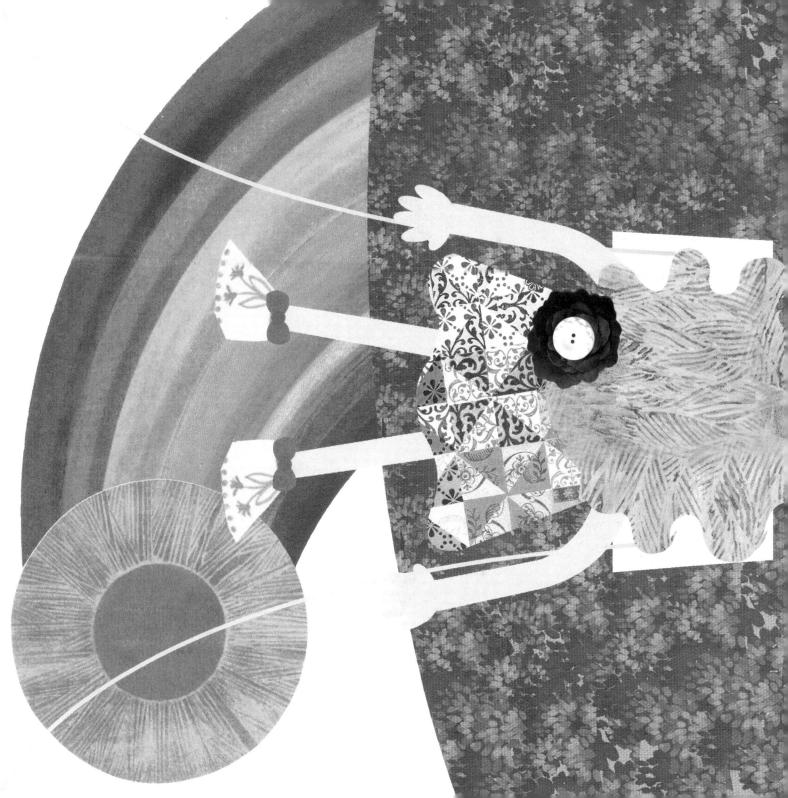

The weight had all gone and now the curls vanished too!

I could run, I could skip, I was feeling brand new.

I grabbed my mum's hand and gave her a grin.

I'm Ruby - that's Who. Outside and in.

CPSIA information can be obtained
at www.ICGtesting.com
Printed in the USA
LVIW011130200912

5254LVAU00002B

9 780987 665300